For my dad, Big Brave Ken, who isn't afraid of anything,
apart from my mum, Little Belligerent Olive.

First published in Great Britain and in the USA in 2007 by
Frances Lincoln Children's Books, 4 Torriano Mews,
Torriano Avenue, London NW5 2RZ

www.franceslincoln.com

First paperback edition published in Great Britain in 2009 and in the USA in 2010

British Library Cataloguing in Publication Data available on request

ISBN: 978-1-84507-995-6

The illustrations in this book are watercolour and black pen

Set in HooskerDont and SpookyOne

Printed in Singapore

3 5 7 9 8 6 4 2

You can find out more about the books by M.P. Robertson
on his website: www.mprobertson.co.uk

BIG BRAVE BRIAN

M.P. Robertson

F

FRANCES LINCOLN
CHILDREN'S BOOKS

Big Brave Brian is the bravest man in the world.

Grumpy Grizzly Bears

that live beneath the stairs
are no match for Big Brave Brian.

Big Brave Brian is not afraid of

Bottom-Biting
Bog Monsters

that terrorize the toilet.

Incy Wincy Spiders

that climb up the spout don't frighten Big Brave Brian.

Slime-Slurpin' Slug Creatures

that drink his bathwater like soup
hold no fear for Brian.

Ghastly Gawping Giants

that stare through
his bedroom window
don't make Brian's
knees knock.

Teddy Gobbling Goblins

that tumble from the toy chest

don't give Brian the collywobbles.

Things that go BUMP in the Night

Sock-Munching Demons

that lurk under the bed
don't scare Big Brave Brian.

But there is one thing that even
Big Brave Brian
is scared of...

MORE TITLES BY M.P. ROBERTSON
FROM FRANCES LINCOLN CHILDREN'S BOOKS

Hieronymus Betts and his Unusual Pets

Hieronymus Betts has some very unusual pets.
But he knows of something that is slimier, noisier, greedier, scarier, and stranger than all of them put together. But what on earth could it be?
Dare you read this book to find out?

Big Foot

There is a creature lurking in the deep, dark woods. Something big... something hairy...
One crisp, bright night a little girl hears his sad song. She follows his huge snowy footprints deep into the darkness of the forest. Cold and shivering, she becomes lost in the falling snow, far from home. Suddenly, from behind a tree, she spies a large, hairy face with gentle eyes. It is Big Foot...

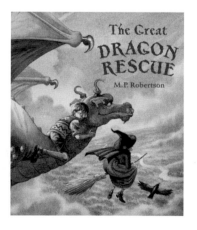

The Great Dragon Rescue

When George's dragon swoops out of the sky and carries him off to a magical land, George knows an adventure has begun. So when he meets a witch who has imprisoned a baby dragon, George thinks up a clever scheme to rescue the baby and reunite it with its dragon dad.

Frances Lincoln titles are available from all good bookshops.
You can also buy books and find out more about your favourite titles, authors and illustrators on our website: www.franceslincoln.com